# Our Wish for You

## A Story About Open Adoption

Dano Moreno

*Illustrated by* Ryan O'Rourke

Charlesbridge

For our son—D. M.

For Kaylee, Riley, and Liam—R. O.

Published by Charlesbridge
9 Galen Street
Watertown, MA 02472
(617) 926-0329
www.charlesbridge.com

Printed in China
(hc) 10 9 8 7 6 5 4 3 2 1

Illustrations done in digital media
Display type hand lettered by Ryan O'Rouke and Jon Simeon
Text type set in ITC Cheltenham by Bertram Goodhue and Ingalls Kimball
Printed by 1010 Printing International Limited in Huizhou, Guangdong, China
Production supervision by Jennifer Most Delaney
Designed by Jon Simeon

**Library of Congress Cataloging-in-Publication Data**
Names: Moreno, Dano, author. | O'Rourke, Ryan, illustrator.
Title: Our wish for you: a story about open adoption / Dano Moreno; illustrated by Ryan O'Rourke.
Description: Watertown, MA: Charlesbridge, [2023] | Audience: Ages 3–7. | Audience: Grades K–1. | Summary: "In a celebration of open adoption, both a baby's birth mother and his adoptive parents share the same universal wishes for the child."—Provided by publisher.
Identifiers: LCCN 2022012742 (print) | LCCN 2022012743 (ebook) | ISBN 9781623543556 (hardcover) | ISBN 9781632893277 (ebook)
Subjects: LCSH: Open adoption—Juvenile fiction. | Adopted children—Juvenile fiction. | Birthmothers—Juvenile fiction. | Adoptive parents—Juvenile fiction. | CYAC: Open adoption—Fiction. | Adoption—Fiction. | Birthmothers—Fiction. | Adoptive parents—Fiction. | LCGFT: Picture books.
Classification: LCC PZ7.1.M669527 Ou 2023 (print) | LCC PZ7.1.M669527 (ebook) | DDC [E]—dc23
LC record available at https://lccn.loc.gov/2022012742
LC ebook record available at https://lccn.loc.gov/2022012743

**B**efore you were born, we wished for you.

We didn't know when you'd come into our lives—or if you ever would.

So we hoped and waited.

Then one day, in your birth mom's womb, you began to grow.

You were smaller than an apple when she discovered she was pregnant.

Yet raising a child felt as big as a mountain.

She took a deep breath and placed a hand on her chest.

Then her heart filled with love—the kind that parents feel.

She made a wish just for you—the kind that parents make.

A wish for giggles throughout the day,

for hugs when there are tears,

SQUEAK....

SQUEAK....

for dreams that lead to new adventures,

for wonder in every step.

But your birth mom didn't feel she could fulfill her wish on her own.

She searched for people who were
ready for a baby.

Who could she trust?
Who would she choose?

Eventually, she found us.

She asked us to adopt you—
to give you what you need to grow.

Above all, she asked that you would
always know how many people love you.

So what did we say?

# Yes, of course!

We wanted the same things for you.

We had waited so long for this moment to arrive.

And soon . . .

. . . you arrived too!

We took a deep breath and each placed a hand on our chest.

Then our hearts filled with love—the kind that parents feel.

We made a wish just for you—the kind that parents make.

A wish for giggles throughout the day,

for hugs when there are tears,

for dreams that lead to new adventures, for wonder in every step.

As you grow, your laughs get louder,

your hugs feel tighter,

and your dreams take flight.

You find wonder in every day,

in tiny treasures . . .

. . . and in grand creations.

And some days feel especially bright.

Some days, our love brings us together. . . .

And together we all see
a wish come true.

# Author's Note

Today, many adoptions in the US are open adoptions. This means that the child, the birth parents, and the adoptive parents (the legal parents) know each other or know about each other. They may talk, write, share photos, or spend time together. It's common for children in adoptive families to ask questions about their birth families—and to have feelings of both joy and sadness related to their adoption. Open adoption can help children get answers to their questions, form a positive view of adoption, and maintain a connection to their birth family and culture.

In closed adoptions, the child and adoptive parents do not interact with the birth parents. People choose closed adoptions for various reasons. Some parents fear that an open adoption would be difficult. Sometimes, a closed adoption is the safest option. And in some places, open adoption is not available or common. Even when an adoption is closed, many children and birth parents search for each other later in life.

My husband and I became fathers through open adoption. When we first explored possible paths to parenthood, it became clear that each of our options would require trust and help from others—and that the same was true for any birth parent who chose adoption. Though we had some worries about welcoming new people into our lives, we felt it was important to honor our son's connection with his birth family. The result has been the same for us and our son: more love.

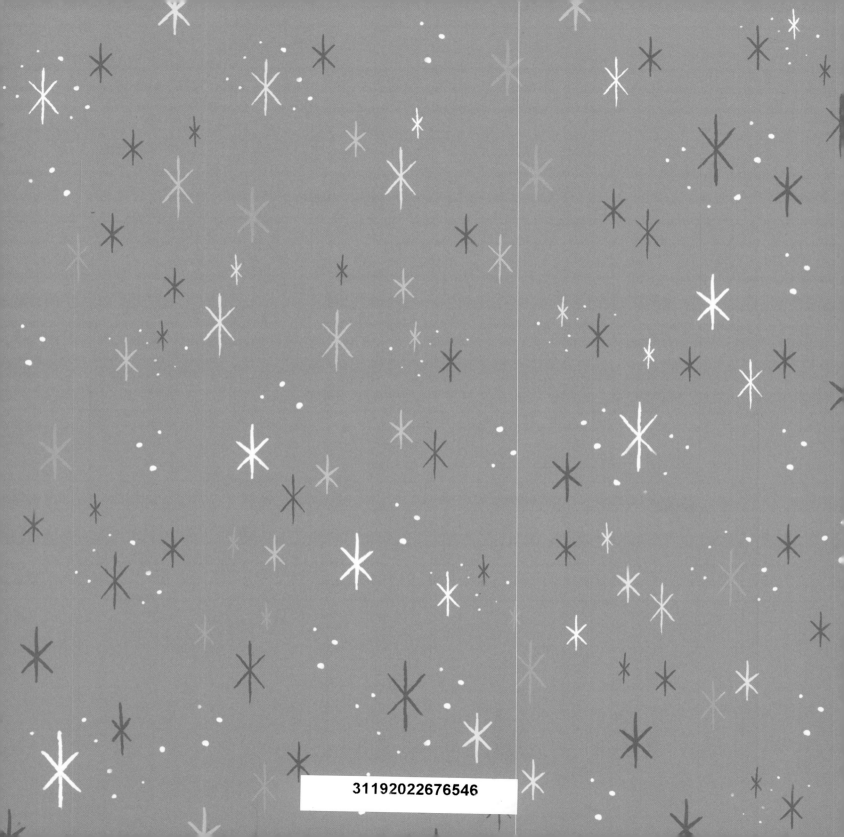